MR. PACK RAT
REALLY WANTS THAT

BY MARCUS EWERT
ILLUSTRATED BY KAYLA STARK

PLUM BLOSSOM
BOOKS

BERKELEY, CALIFORNIA

PLUM BLOSSOM BOOKS

Plum Blossom Books, the children's imprint of Parallax Press, publishes books on mindfulness for young people and the grown-ups in their lives.

Parallax Press
P.O. Box 7355
Berkeley, CA 94707
parallax.org

Story © 2018 Marcus Ewert
Illustrations © 2018 Kayla Stark

Parallax Press is the publishing division of Plum Village Community of Engaged Buddhism, Inc.

Printed in Malaysia

ISBN: 978-1-946764-25-6

Cover and text design by Debbie Berne

Library of Congress Cataloging-in-Publication Data

Names: Ewert, Marcus, author. | Stark, Kayla, illustrator.
Title: Mr. Pack Rat really wants that! / Marcus Ewert; illustrated by Kayla Stark.
Description: Berkeley, CA : Parallax Press, [2018] | Summary: "Through trial and error, Mr. Pack Rat begins to question whether having more things is really the secret to happiness" —Provided by publisher.
Identifiers: LCCN 2018010890 | ISBN 9781946764256 (hardback)
Subjects: | CYAC: Collectors and collecting—Fiction. | Belongings, Personal—Fiction. | Magic—Fiction. | Wood rats—Fiction. | Contentment—Fiction. | BISAC: JUVENILE FICTION / Animals / Mice, Hamsters, Guinea Pigs, etc.. | JUVENILE FICTION / Social Issues / Self-Esteem & Self-Reliance. | JUVENILE FICTION / Social Issues / Manners & Etiquette.
Classification: LCC PZ7.E94717 Mr 2018 | DDC [E]—dc23
LC record available at https://lccn.loc.gov/2018010890

1 2 3 4 5 / 22 21 20 19 18

FSC
www.fsc.org

MIX
Paper from
responsible sources
FSC® C012700

For Derek Spreckelmeyer, friend, roommate,
and de-clutterer extraordinaire.

Mr. Pack Rat felt so good, he thought he might explode.

He had just built his first *midden!*

What's a midden?

It's a nest pack rats build out of whatever's lying around.

Mr. Pack Rat's midden had a theme: BROWN.

He'd gathered

brown pine needles

brown sticks and leaves

brown acorns, pinecones, and chips of bark.

"Brown is such a cozy color!" Mr. Pack Rat said.
"And *my* midden is the brownest midden *ever!*"

"Whew!" he said. "I need a break!"

So he walked to his favorite meadow.

The wildflowers were all in bloom.

"Oh, these COLORS!" he gasped. "Juicy reds, perky oranges, and lemony yellows! It's like a rainbow fell from the sky and broke into a million pieces!"

He thought of his midden. "Ugh!" he cried. "A one-color midden is so *boring*! Only these COLORS can make me happy!"

Mr. Pack Rat had an old metal bar that had been in his family a long, long time. The bar didn't look like much, but with the right words, it worked like a magnet—a *magical* magnet!

He pointed the bar at the flowers, and said:

All these flowers that I see,
Magnet, bring them home with me!
Mr. Pack Rat,
Mr. Pack Rat,
Mr. Pack Rat really wants that!

KLINNNG!

The bar rang like a bell.

The magic jumped out and—fft! fft! fft!—plucked every flower.

Mr. Pack Rat marched home, with the flowers bobbing behind him.

Mr. Pack Rat was delighted with his colorful midden . . . for about a week. But then the flowers did what flowers do: they withered and turned brown. Mr. Pack Rat was back to a one-color midden! (And the dead flowers kind of stank.)

"EWWWW!" he cried. "I'm going OUT!"

He walked to his favorite beach.

That day, the waves had pushed their most beautiful shells onto the sand.

"Such glittering shapes and forms!" Mr. Pack Rat gushed. "It's like a million pirates emptied their treasure chests onto the beach! And SHELLS don't wilt!"

Pointing the bar, he said:

Seashells that the ocean gave,
Magnet, drag them to my cave!
Mr. Pack Rat,
Mr. Pack Rat,
Mr. Pack Rat really wants that!

The bar rang: **KLANNGGGG!**

The magic jumped out and—*rackle rackle rackle!*—scooped up every shell.

Mr. Pack Rat strode home.

The shells jostled noisily behind him.

Mr. Pack Rat was truly happy . . . for a couple of hours.

But away from the sun, sand, and sea, the shells didn't dazzle.

And what can you really *do* with shells, anyway? Sort them?

#3 SHELL   #1 SHELL   #2 SHELL

"ARGHH!" Mr. Pack Rat shouted. "You shells are so boring! I'm going OUT!"

He walked to his favorite store.

Everywhere he looked, there was something cool.

"Toys and tools and games!" he cried. "Telescopes and fishing rods! It's like a million scientists invented every fun thing they could think of! I WANT IT ALL!"

The bar was already in his hand.

*I have **lots** but I want **MORE**!*
Magnet, EMPTY every store!
Mr. Pack Rat,
Mr. Pack Rat,
Mr. Pack Rat really wants that!

KLONGGGG!

The bar rang *very* loudly.

The magic picked every item up and—***schwizz!
schwizz! schwizz!***—*threw* it at Mr. Pack Rat.

This time he had to *run* home, to keep
from getting clonked on the head!

Mr. Pack Rat's cave was so cluttered that there wasn't room for him to play with his new belongings.

There was barely enough room for *him*!

"Eeep!" he squeaked. "I can't *breathe*!"

He just managed to *squeeeeze* outside.

Stars flared against the jet-black sky.

"Infinite space!" he cried. "Majestic vastness!
IWANTITIWANTITIWANTIT!!!"

I don't see a reason why
I shouldn't own THE WHOLE NIGHT SKY!
Mr. Pack Rat,
Mr. Pack Rat,
Mr. Pack Rat really wants that!

KLUNGGGG!

The bar rang like a gong of doom.

The magic *tugged* every star, moon, and planet.

A comet headed straight for Mr. Pack Rat!

"No no no!" he shrieked. "I take it back! I DON'T want the whole night sky! Please, Magnet, *I take back my wish*!"

The bar leapt out of his hands.

When it finally fell, it hit the ground with a **THUDDD**.

Everything was quiet.

The moon, stars, and planets sat in their proper places.

The comet headed somewhere else.

Mr. Pack Rat threw himself on the ground.

"I was almost *squashed*!" he wailed. "How did everything go so wrong? I just wanted to be happy."

He cried and cried, until he finally fell asleep.

When Mr. Pack Rat woke up the next morning,
the sun was as yellow as fresh butter.

Breezes chased each other in the grass.

Every leaf wore crystals of morning dew.

"Ahhhhh," said Mr. Pack Rat. He was smiling.

He immediately reached for the bar.

But then he stopped.

"No no no, Mr. Pack Rat," he said. "What were you going to wish for, the sun?"

Mr. Pack Rat sat down in a pretty glade.

Sunshine warmed his face.

Breezes tickled his fur.

Butterflies danced in the air around him.

Mr. Pack Rat was . . . *happy*.

He looked at the metal bar.

"You know, Magnet," he said at last. "I've been using you all wrong. I kept asking you for things to MAKE me happy. But I never knew when I was happy ALREADY."

"And actually, I'm happy quite a lot of the time! What I need is a *friend*, to remind me of that!"

The bar began ringing merrily: ***klinga-ding, klinga-ding!***

"What is it, Magnet?" said Mr. Pack Rat. "You sound so happ-."

Mr. Pack Rat stopped. Then he giggled. "Oh!" he said. "I get it!"

KLINGA-DING!

From then on, the bar rang—***klinga-ding, klinga-ding***—whenever Mr. Pack Rat was already happy.

Klinga-ding-ding it rang, when Mr. Pack Rat returned everything to the store, and he saw the smile on the shopkeeper's face.

Klinga-ding-ding it rang when
Mr. Pack Rat brought the shells
back to the beach, and rearranged
them on the sand.

Klinga-ding! rang the bar when Mr. Pack Rat
spread the dead flowers all over the meadow.
The dead flowers would become mulch from
which new flowers would spring.

And *klinga-ding, klinga-ding* rang the bar very softly,
when Mr. Pack Rat curled up on his brown midden,
ready for a good night's sleep.

Mr. Pack Rat,
Mr. Pack Rat,
Mr. Pack Rat really likes that!

PLUM BLOSSOM
BOOKS

Plum Blossom Books, the children's
imprint of Parallax Press, publishes
books on mindfulness for young people
and the grown-ups in their lives.

For a copy of the catalog, please contact:

Parallax Press
P.O. Box 7355
Berkeley, CA 94707

parallax.org

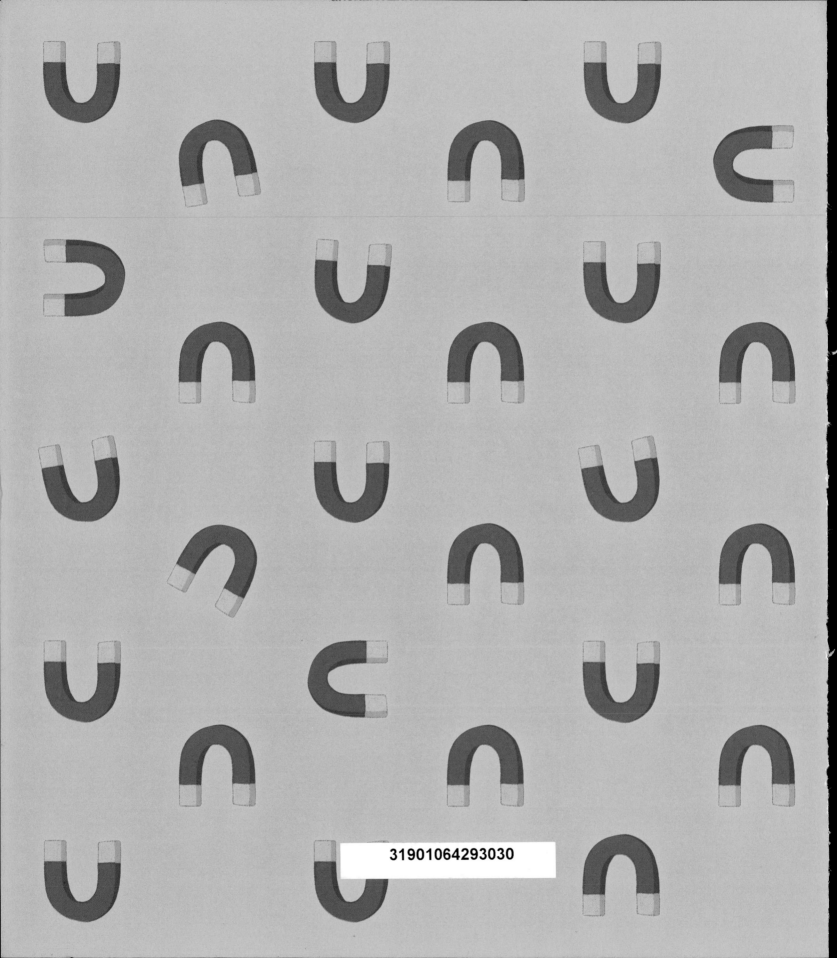